My dearest pup

I hope this letter reaches you safe and sound. You have been so brave since you had to flee from the evil wolf Shadow.

Do not worry about me. I will hide here until you are strong enough to return and lead our pack. For now you must move on – you must hide from Shadow and his spies. If Shadow finds this letter I believe he will try to destroy it . . .

Find a good friend – someone to help finish my message to you. Because what I have to say to you is important. What I have to say is this: you must always

Please don't feel lonely. Trust in your friends and all will be well.

Your loving mother,

Canista

Sue Bentley's books for children often include animals, fairies and wildlife. She lives in Northampton and enjoys reading, going to the cinema, relaxing by her garden pond and watching the birds feeding their babies on the lawn. At school she was always getting told off for daydreaming or staring out of the window – but she now realizes that she was storing up ideas for when she became a writer. She has met and owned many cats and dogs, and each one has brought a special kind of magic to her life.

Sue Bentley

Magic Puppy

A New Beginning

Illustrated by *Angela Swan*

PUFFIN

To Cindy – first and best-beloved,
who was happy in a doll's pram

PUFFIN BOOKS

Published by the Penguin Group
Penguin Books Ltd, 80 Strand, London WC2R ORL, England
Penguin Group (USA) Inc., 375 Hudson Street, New York, New York 10014, USA
Penguin Group (Canada), 90 Eglinton Avenue East, Suite 700, Toronto, Ontario, Canada M4P 2Y3
(a division of Pearson Penguin Canada Inc.)
Penguin Ireland, 25 St Stephen's Green, Dublin 2, Ireland (a division of Penguin Books Ltd)
Penguin Group (Australia), 250 Camberwell Road, Camberwell, Victoria 3124, Australia
(a division of Pearson Australia Group Pty Ltd)
Penguin Books India Pvt Ltd, 11 Community Centre, Panchsheel Park, New Delhi – 110 017, India
Penguin Group (NZ), 67 Apollo Drive, Rosedale, North Shore 0632, New Zealand
(a division of Pearson New Zealand Ltd)
Penguin Books (South Africa) (Pty) Ltd, 24 Sturdee Avenue, Rosebank,
Johannesburg 2196, South Africa

Penguin Books Ltd, Registered Offices: 80 Strand, London WC2R ORL, England

puffinbooks.com

First published 2008
13

Text copyright © Sue Bentley, 2008
Illustrations copyright © Angela Swan, 2008
All rights reserved

The moral right of the author and illustrator has been asserted

Set in Bembo
Typeset by Palimpsest Book Production Limited, Grangemouth, Stirlingshire
Made and printed in England by Clays Ltd, St Ives plc

British Library Cataloguing in Publication Data
A CIP catalogue record for this book is available from the British Library

ISBN: 978-0-141-32350-3

www.greenpenguin.co.uk

Prologue

Storm whimpered as he crawled into
the cave. Behind the young silver-grey
wolf, stars glimmered in the purple sky.

Suddenly, a piercing howl echoed on
the night air.

'Shadow!' Storm gasped, trembling
with fear.

The fierce lone wolf who had
attacked the Moon-claw pack was close

by. Storm must disguise himself, and quickly!

There was a dazzling gold flash and a fountain of golden sparks that lit up the back of the cave for a brief second. Where the wolf cub had stood, there now crouched a tiny, sandy golden retriever puppy with floppy ears and twinkling midnight-blue eyes.

Storm's little puppy heart beat fast. In that split second of light, he had seen the she-wolf lying crumpled against a rock.

'Mother?' he whined, plunging deeper into the cave.

'Storm?' Canista lifted her head to answer him in a velvety growl.

In the dim light Storm could see his

mother's heaving sides and hear her rapid breathing. He felt a new surge of panic. 'You are hurt! Did Shadow attack you too?'

Canista nodded weakly. 'His bite is poisoned. It drains my strength.'

Storm's blue eyes flared with sorrow and anger. 'He has already killed my father and my three litter brothers. I will face Shadow and fight him!'

'Bravely said, my son. But now is not the time. You are the only cub left of our Moon-claw pack. Go to the other world. Use this disguise to hide. Return when your magic is stronger. Then, together, we will fight Shadow.' Canista's head flopped back tiredly as she finished speaking.

Storm bowed his head. He did not

want to leave her, but he knew his mother was right.

The sound of mighty paws and a thunderous snarl echoed from the mouth of the cave.

'Go, Storm. Save yourself,' Canista growled urgently.

Storm's sandy fur ignited with gold sparks. He whined softly as he felt the power building inside him. The golden light around him grew brighter. And brighter . . .

Chapter ONE

Lily Benson felt a leap of excitement as her dad drew up outside Greengates riding stables.

'Yay! I love Saturday afternoons. I get to spend hours and hours with ponies!' she cried, jumping out of the car.

Lily went round to the open window and bent down to kiss her dad's cheek.

Mr Benson laughed. 'Careful you don't get pony-overload!'

'There's no such thing,' Lily said firmly. Her bedroom walls were covered with posters of ponies and her bookcase was crammed with riding books and magazines.

'Shame. I was hoping you might stop pestering your mum and me to buy you one!' her dad said.

He was only joking, but Lily felt a pang. She was desperate for a pony of her own. But her parents were worried about the hard work and amount of time it would take to look after it. Lily knew they were hoping she'd be satisfied with having free rides in exchange for helping out at Greengates.

'I'll never stop asking in a zillion years. Ponies rule, Dad!' she said.

'You've got a one-track mind, Lily Benson. Have a good time. See you later,' he called, steering away from the kerb.

Lily sighed. She waved goodbye and then went into the stable yard.

The main stable buildings were built around two sides of a square. A large gate at one end led to the paddock. Just beyond the paddock Lily could see the cottage where Janie Green who ran Greengates lived.

Janie was outside the tack room with Treacle and Taffy, two of the smaller ponies. Two young children in riding gear stood waiting ready to mount.

Janie looked up and smiled warmly as

Lily approached. She had a round pretty face with twinkling brown eyes and was always cheerful. 'Hi, Lily. I hope you're feeling energetic. We're fully booked this afternoon.'

'Hi, Janie,' Lily said. She patted Taffy's neck and stroked Treacle's nose. 'What do you want me to do first?'

'You could give Don a hand with the mucking out, if you don't mind. He's over at Bandit's stall,' Janie said.

'OK,' Lily said happily. Bandit was her favourite pony. She was a sweet-natured palomino with a golden-tan coat and a pale mane and tail. Lily would have loved to own a pony just like her.

As Lily went off to find the stable lad she saw even more young riders arriving with their parents. It looked

like it was going to be a hectic
afternoon.

Lily said hello to Bandit for a few
minutes, before spending the next hour
or so forking up droppings, wheeling
them over to the muck heap and
spreading fresh bedding.

Riders and ponies came and went.

Lily lent a hand where it was needed. It was a hot day and she was soon red-faced and sweaty.

'Why don't you take a break and go and get a drink?' Don suggested, as she helped him fill the hay nets and water buckets. He was tall and wiry, with dark-red hair, freckles and a thin face.

'Phew! I think I will,' Lily said, pushing a strand of damp blonde hair back from her forehead.

She went to the stable's kitchen and had a long, cold drink of orange juice.

As Lily was sauntering back past the paddock, she noticed some litter blowing about on the grass and went to pick it up.

'Thanks for that, Lily. You're doing a grand job!' Janie Green called, pausing

to rest the heavy saddle she was
carrying on the paddock fence.

'It makes me so mad when people
leave stuff about. Don't they care that a
plastic bag could kill a pony if it eats
it?' Lily said indignantly.

'I don't suppose they give it a
thought. Maybe they'd be more careful
if they did — but not everyone's into
horses.'

Lily shrugged. 'That's their loss, then!'

'I'm with you on that!' Janie said,
smiling. 'Have you persuaded your
parents to buy you a pony yet?'

Lily pulled a face, thinking miserably
of the earlier conversation with her
dad.

'I take it that's a sore point,' Janie said.

Lily nodded. 'I still have to convince

them that I can fit looking after a pony round my schoolwork. Mum and Dad think it would be too much for me and I should wait until I'm older.'

'They could be right, you know,' Janie said gently. 'Looking after a pony is a big commitment and there are no days off.'

Lily felt her spirits sink. She'd thought Janie would be on her side!

'How do you fancy taking Bandit out? We've just had a cancellation, so she's free for a couple of hours,' Janie said.

Lily brightened immediately at the thought of a longer free ride than usual. 'Really? I can take her out by myself?' she asked delightedly.

Janie nodded. 'You've ridden her

plenty of times and she's used to you.
You can take her along the bridle
paths, but don't go beyond the woods.
OK?'

Lily nodded, feeling proud that
Janie trusted her. 'Thanks, Janie! That's
brilliant!'

She dashed straight across to Bandit,
who was already tacked up. 'Hello, girl.
We're going for a ride,' she crooned,
stroking the pony's nose.

Bandit gave a friendly whicker and
nuzzled Lily's palm. Lily buckled on
her riding hat before mounting the
palomino pony and using her heels to
nudge her forward.

They trotted out of Greengates and
turned on to the bridle path that ran
down the edge of a field. The path

branched further on and Lily took the
way to the woods.

Other riders from the stables passed
her on their way back.

As she and Bandit entered the shade
of the trees, Lily's mind drifted into a
wonderful daydream. It was easy to
imagine that Bandit was her own pony
and they were quite alone. The sound
of other riders was muffled and she was

screened from them by the thick
bushes. Sunlight filtered through the
leaves and speckled everything with
spots of light.

'I wish you were mine,' Lily said
dreamily, leaning forward to pat Bandit's
satiny neck.

Suddenly Bandit stumbled on a tree
root and the reins were jerked right out
of Lily's hands.

'Oh!' Lily pitched forward and shot
straight over the pony's neck. As the
ground rushed up to meet her she
closed her eyes, ready for the painful
landing.

Chapter
TWO

The collision with the ground never
came.

With a dazzling golden flash and a
crackle of sparks, Lily found herself
jerking to a sudden halt. Her eyes flew
open in shock and she saw that she was
caught inside a huge glowing golden
net, in mid-air, half a metre above the
ground!

Very slowly, Lily felt herself float
down and land gently on some bracken.
With a fizzing noise, the glowing net
broke up into golden sparks and then
melted away into the leaves.

Lily sat up, blinking confusedly.
Her first thought was for Bandit. She
whipped round and was relieved to see
the pony nibbling some grass in a small
clearing a few metres away.

'Your riding creature is fine. I hope
that you are not injured,' said a strange
voice.

Lily stiffened. 'W-who said that?'

A tiny puppy with sandy fur, floppy
ears and huge midnight-blue eyes
crawled out from beneath a frond of
bracken. 'I did. My name is Storm of
the Moon-claw pack. What are you?

And what is the name of your pack?' it woofed.

Lily's jaw dropped as she stared at the puppy in utter amazement. She felt like pinching herself to make sure she wasn't dreaming. But she saw that the puppy was looking at her quizzically as if waiting for her to respond.

'I'm a g-girl. A human . . . I'm L-Lily. Lily Benson,' she found herself

stammering. 'But I don't know what you mean about a pack.'

'A human? I have heard of these.' Storm's silky forehead wrinkled in a frown. Lily saw that he was beginning to tremble. 'Can I trust you, Lily? I come from far away and I need your help.'

Lily was still having difficulty taking this in, but she didn't want to frighten this amazing puppy away. He was absolutely gorgeous with the brightest midnight-blue eyes she had ever seen and big soft paws that looked too big for his body.

Very slowly she got up on to her knees and reached out her hand.

To Lily's delight, Storm edged closer and brushed her fingers with his damp little nose. His tail wagged nervously.

Despite being so scared, the tiny puppy seemed to trust her.

'Why do you need my help?' she asked gently.

Storm's deep-blue eyes flashed with anger and sadness. 'A lone wolf called Shadow attacked us. My father and brothers were killed and my mother is sick and in hiding. Shadow wants to lead the Moon-claw wolf pack, but the others will not follow him as long as I am alive.'

'*Wolf* pack? But you're a pup—' Lily stopped as Storm held up a velvety sandy paw and began backing away.

There was another dazzling bright flash and a burst of gold sparks showered over Lily, crackling around her feet on the ground.

'Oh!' Lily rubbed her eyes, blinded
for a second. When she could see again,
she saw that the tiny sandy puppy had
gone. In its place now stood a majestic
young wolf with thick silver-grey fur
and glowing midnight-blue eyes.

'Storm?' Lily gasped, eyeing the wolf's
large teeth and thick neck-ruff that
glimmered with hundreds of gold sparks
like tiny yellow diamonds.

'Yes, Lily, it is me,' Storm said in a
deep velvety growl.

Before Lily could get used to seeing Storm as his magnificent real self, there was a final gold flash and he appeared once again as a cute sandy puppy.

'Wow! You really are a wolf. That's a brilliant disguise,' she said, getting up from her knees.

Storm began trembling again. 'Not if Shadow's magic finds me. Will you help me to hide?'

Lily's heart went out to the helpless puppy. 'Of course I will. You can live with . . .' She tailed off as she remembered her parents' rules about having no house pets as they were out all day. They'd probably insist on taking Storm to the pet care centre. There must be some way she could help the tiny puppy. 'Maybe I could smuggle you into my house, but I don't see how I can hide you for long,' she said thoughtfully.

'Do not worry. I will use my magic so that only you will be able to see and hear me,' Storm woofed.

'You can make yourself invisible? Wow!' Lily breathed. 'No problem, then. You're coming straight home with me. Just let me catch Bandit. By the time

we get back to Greengates, it'll be time for Dad to pick me up.'

A few minutes later, as she cradled Storm in her lap on Bandit's back, a big smile spread across Lily's face. Never in her wildest dreams had she imagined having a magic puppy for a friend!

Chapter
THREE

'You should sleep in here in case Mum or Dad gets suspicious,' Lily told Storm, spreading an old jumper in the bottom of her wardrobe. 'But when no one's around, you can get on my bed.'

Storm looked in the wardrobe and then padded around her bedroom, sniffing everything and exploring. 'This is a good place.'

'Glad you like it!' Lily said, beaming at him. 'Are you hungry?'

The tiny puppy barked eagerly.

'OK. I'll go and raid the kitchen to see what I can find. I won't be long.'

Lily dashed downstairs. Luckily her dad was in the garden cutting the lawn and her mum had just gone out to her yoga class. She found some leftover chicken in the fridge and quickly broke a piece off for Storm.

Back upstairs, she watched as Storm ate hungrily and then sat back licking his lips. 'That was delicious. I like human food.'

'I'll get you some proper food later,' Lily said.

Storm nodded. 'Good. We will go hunting together!'

'I couldn't do that!' Lily said,
horrified. 'Anyway, there's no need. The
shop at the end of the street sells dog
food in tins. I'll buy some with my
pocket money,' she told him.

Storm yawned, showing his sharp
little teeth. 'I think that I will rest now.'
Padding over to the wardrobe, he curled
up on the old jumper with a contented
sigh and promptly went to sleep.

Lily watched the tiny puppy's furry

sides rising and falling. Almost at once his paws twitched as he started dreaming. *He must be exhausted from his long journey*, she thought, already feeling fond of him.

Leaving Storm to sleep, Lily reached for a book of pony stories and stretched out on her tummy on her bed to read.

The book was really good and she hardly noticed time passing. She was halfway through an exciting story about a pony being stolen, when something leapt on to her bed and launched itself on top of her.

Lily almost jumped out of her skin. 'Storm! You scared me!' she said, laughing as she rolled over on to her back. 'Did you have a good snooze?'

'Yes, thank you. I feel safe here with you,' Storm woofed happily. Plonking his big soft paws on her book, he leaned up and began licking her chin.

Lily wrapped her arms round his plump little sandy body and gave him a cuddle. After a couple of minutes, Storm squirmed free and sprang on to the rug with a surprisingly loud thud for a tiny puppy.

'I would like to go outside now!'

'OK,' Lily said, getting up off the bed. 'Our garden's not very big, but there's a field nearby. I'll take you for a walk over there.'

Storm gave an eager little bark and followed her downstairs.

As they reached the hall, her dad appeared at the sitting-room door. He had a frown on his face. 'What was all that thumping about upstairs? It sounded like a herd of elephants.'

'Dad! I . . . er . . . thought you were outside,' Lily gasped in panic.

She quickly shifted about, trying to stand in front of Storm before she suddenly remembered that he was invisible. Then, realizing how strange that must look, she began bending and stretching her arms. 'Whew! Whew!'

she puffed for added emphasis. 'Just
doing a few exercises. I'm trying to get
fit. I was about to come and tell you
that I'm going out for a jog around the
field!'

Her dad raised his eyebrows as Lily
did a star jump. 'Well, I guess that's a
good idea. Maybe I'll come with you.
I could do with some exercise too.'

'No!' Lily said hastily. 'Someone . . .
um . . . from school might see me. I'll

look a real baby if I'm trailing around after you.'

'Pardon me for trying to cramp your style,' her dad joked. 'What's brought this new fitness fad on?'

'I want to be ready for when I get my own pony, don't I? It's going to be hard work looking after it,' Lily replied cheekily.

Her dad rolled his eyes. 'I might have known what was at the bottom of this! Do you ever think of anything else beside ponies?'

'Nope! Well, actually, yes! But you wouldn't believe me if I told you!' Lily said, glancing at Storm who was waiting by the front door. She jogged towards him before her dad could ask any more awkward questions. 'See you later!'

Chapter
FOUR

As Lily put her school books into her
bag on Monday morning, Storm sat
watching her.

She smiled at him. 'I love having you
living here with me, but I have to go
out for a few hours. Try not to get
bored and chew my rug or anything,
or Mum will freak!'

'I will not do anything like that,'
Storm yapped indignantly.

'Sorry. Sometimes I forget you're not
an ordinary puppy,' Lily said, bending
down to stroke his silky ears. 'It's a
shame there was only time for a
quick walk around the field before
breakfast. I'll take you out for a
mega-long walk when I get back
from school. Promise.'

Storm looked up at her curiously.
'What is school?'

'It's a place where kids go to learn.
Teachers tell us stuff and give us
homework to do and we do projects
and all kinds of things,' Lily explained.

'School sounds interesting. I will
come with you,' Storm decided.

Lily grinned. 'I wish you could, but pets
aren't allowed . . .' She paused as she had
a second thought. 'Hey! Maybe you *can*
come if you stay invisible! But you'd have
to keep really quiet and stay close to me.
Mr Poke, our class teacher, is very strict.'

Storm's face brightened and his
little sandy tail started wagging with
excitement. 'I will make sure that no one
will know I'm there – except you, Lily!'

'Cool! Let's go!' Lily put her school

bag on the floor and opened it up. 'It might be best if you got inside. I have to cross some busy roads.'

Storm jumped into her bag and settled next to her books and gym kit. Lily shouldered her bag, said goodbye to her parents and headed out of the front door.

'We'll probably meet Freema and Katy, my friends from class, on the way. I can't wait to see their faces when I tell them about you!' she said to Storm.

There was a scuffling noise from her bag. Storm popped his head out, his big dewy eyes looking into Lily's. 'You cannot tell anyone my secret. Promise me, Lily,' he woofed seriously.

Lily was disappointed. She had always

wanted a pet to tell her friends about,
especially a pony, but she had been
really excited at the thought that she
might be able to share her amazing
magic puppy friend. She'd do anything
if it would help keep Storm safe,
though. 'OK, I promise. Cross my heart
and hope to die,' she said.

Storm nodded, satisfied.

As Lily and Storm reached the school
gate, they saw Freema and Katy. There
was another girl with them whom Lily
hadn't seen before.

'Hi, Katy. Hi, Freema,' Lily greeted
her friends.

'Hi, Lily. This is my cousin, Adjoa,'
Freema explained. 'She's just moved
here and is going to be in our class.'

Adjoa was tall with springy black hair,

an oval face and big brown eyes, just like Freema.

Lily smiled at her. 'Welcome to our school, Adjoa.'

'Thanks,' Adjoa said shyly.

'Did you help out at Greengates this weekend?' Katy asked Lily as they walked into the school grounds.

Lily nodded. 'It was great. I had an extra-long ride on Bandit. Janie let me take her up to the woods by myself.'

'Cool!' Katy said.

'Do you like riding?' Adjoa asked Lily.

'It's my favourite thing ever in the whole world!' Lily replied. 'How about you?'

'Adjoa's pony-mad,' Freema said. She nudged her cousin. 'Tell Lily about your pony.'

Lily's eyes widened. 'You've got your own pony? You lucky thing! What's its name?'

'Pixie. She's gorgeous and I love her to bits,' Adjoa said. 'You can come round one night after school and meet her if you like.'

'Thanks. I'd love to,' Lily said, beaming.

In the classroom, Lily took her usual seat next to Katy. She put her bag on the floor, so that Storm could jump out.

Storm gave himself a shake and then trotted off to sniff around the room.

Mr Poke took the register. 'And just before we begin,' he said, looking up, 'I'd like to welcome Adjoa Hardiker to the class.'

Adjoa smiled shyly as everyone clapped, including Lily.

A few minutes later, Lily was leaning over to watch Storm. She smiled to herself as the tiny puppy weaved in and out of the desks, his sandy tail wagging.

A voice called out, but Lily was engrossed by Storm's cute antics.

'Lily Benson, can you stop daydreaming and take out your history book, please?' the teacher's sarcastic voice said. Mr Poke had a bald head with a fuzzy rim of hair round his ears. He had a way of looking down his nose when he was annoyed.

Lily's head snapped up. 'Sorry, sir.'

'Looks like old Poker Face got out of bed the wrong side – again,' Katy commented. Adjoa and Freema, who sat nearby, giggled.

Lily turned round and grinned at them.

'Right, class. I'd like you to begin work on your projects, please. Quietly, if possible!' Mr Poke ordered.

They were doing the Tudors. Lily was making a collage of Queen Elizabeth I. 'I think I'll do her lace ruff today. I need to get some bits of paper and stuff from the art cupboard,' she said to Katy, who was bent over writing in her notebook.

'Can we have a bit more work and a little less talking, Lily Benson?' Mr Poke drawled.

'Yes, sir.' Lily felt herself going pink as she got up and went to the cupboard. *I wasn't even doing anything*, she thought.

Storm padded over to her. 'Are you all right, Lily? You look hot,' he woofed.

'I'm fine. Not like *some* people,' Lily murmured, glancing back at the grumpy teacher.

She pulled the cupboard's handle, but it seemed to have stuck. Grasping it more firmly, she pulled again, but the door still wouldn't budge.

'I will help,' Storm yapped eagerly.

Lily saw Mr Poke coming over with a frown on his face. 'Uh-oh, you'd better be quick, Storm. Looks like Poker Face is on the war path,' she whispered.

Lily felt an odd, warm tingling down her spine as gold sparks ignited in Storm's sandy coat, and the tips of his ears and tail fizzed with power. Something strange was going to happen.

Raising one big sandy front paw, Storm sent a shower of bright golden sparks whooshing towards the cupboard. With a faint crackle they sank into the wood. For a moment nothing happened and Lily thought Storm's magic hadn't worked.

'Out of the way, Lily. Let me do it,' Mr Poke said irritably, reaching the cupboard — just as the doors sprang open.

An explosion of papers, brushes, pens and paints shot out. Mr Poke flew backwards as if he'd been blown by a wind machine and landed on the floor on his backside.

Rustle! Papers floated down around him. *Splat!* A plastic pot of glue hit Mr Poke on the chest, bursting and spreading all over his grey jumper.

Thwack! Brushes, pens and pencils pinged at him, sticking firmly to the glue.

The teacher sat there blinking in shock.

The whole class erupted with laughter. Katy, Adjoa and Freema were helpless.

Lily tried hard to bite back the laugh bubbling up inside her.

'Whoever packed the cupboard like

that?' Mr Poke roared, his face bright red as he scrambled to his feet. 'I'll have to go and get cleaned up. Get on with your work, class. I'll be right back.' He stomped off towards the cloakroom, shedding pens and pencils with a clatter as he went.

'I am sorry, Lily. I think I used too much magic,' Storm woofed in dismay.

Making sure that no one was looking, Lily quickly patted him. 'You did just fine. It serves Mr Poke right!'

She began putting everything back into the cupboard. Katy, Freema and Adjoa helped her. By the time Mr Poke reappeared wearing a hideous orange, yellow and brown striped T-shirt, the mess was all cleared up.

The rest of the morning passed
quickly, and at lunchtime Lily shared
her cheese sandwiches and crisps with
Storm. When they'd eaten, she took him
for a run across the playing fields. The
excited puppy tore about, chasing leaves
in the wind and tiring himself out. He
spent the rest of the afternoon dozing
under Lily's chair.

After school, with Storm once again
in her bag, Lily walked home with her
friends.

She paused at the end of her road.
'Did you mean it about me coming
round to see Pixie?' she asked Adjoa.

Adjoa nodded. 'Why don't you come
round after school on Friday? We can
both ride Pixie if you like.'

'That would be brilliant!' Lily said.

She jotted Adjoa's address and phone number in her notebook before heading for home. 'Bye. See you all tomorrow!' she called.

Katy, Freema and Adjoa waved as they walked away.

Just inside her front garden, Lily put her bag down so that Storm could jump out. 'Adjoa's nice, isn't she?' she said to him. 'I can't wait to meet Pixie.'

'Me too!' Storm nodded, his pink tongue lolling in a doggy grin.

Lily felt a surge of affection for him. She picked Storm up and stroked his soft sandy fur. 'Having you at school today was brilliant! You really taught old Poker Face a lesson. I hope that horrible Shadow never finds you and then you can live with me forever and come to school every day,' she said.

'That is not possible, Lily,' Storm told her, his small sandy face suddenly serious. 'One day I must return to my own world to help heal my mother and fight Shadow.'

Lily knew this was true, but she didn't want to believe it. She pushed all thoughts of Storm having to leave from her mind and thought instead of the fun they would have on Friday with Adjoa and Pixie.

Chapter
FIVE

'Here you are, girl.' Lily held a piece of carrot on the flat of her hand, so that Pixie could take it with her soft lips. Pixie was a chestnut pony with a white blaze down her nose and a friendly expression.

Lily turned to Adjoa as the pony crunched the treat. 'Pixie's absolutely gorgeous!'

Adjoa smiled. 'I know. I'm lucky to have her.'

Pixie whinnied softly and swivelled her ears.

'I think she agrees with you,' Lily said. They both laughed.

Adjoa opened the field gate and Lily helped her saddle the pony and then both girls spent a happy couple of hours taking it in turns to ride her. Lily thought with a sigh how wonderful it would be to have her own pony and ride her every day.

Storm bounded alongside the pony at first as Lily trotted around the field on her, but his short legs soon got tired. Lily couldn't lift him into her lap with Adjoa watching. 'Are you OK? You're not getting bored?' she leaned down to whisper to him.

'I am fine. I will go and explore,' Storm barked softly.

Lily watched him go gambolling off towards the open-sided, wooden shelter at the bottom of the field. She could see him sniffing all the interesting smells in patches of long grass on the way.

With Storm happily occupied, Lily went back to enjoying her ride. Afterwards she helped Adjoa untack Pixie and then rub her down before letting her run free. The pony immediately threw herself on to her back and had a good roll. Storm ran straight up to her barking happily.

'Oh no!' Lily gasped, only just
stopping herself from calling out to
warn Storm to be careful. If Pixie
kicked out, the tiny puppy could get
badly hurt by her hooves.

'What's wrong?' Adjoa asked, frowning.

'Er . . . nothing,' Lily murmured,
watching tensely as Pixie got to her
feet again and shook herself. Her ears
flattened as she looked down at the
playful puppy, then she leaned down
and gently snuffled Storm's sandy fur.
Storm yapped delightedly, wagging his
tail.

Lily gave a big sigh of relief, which she quickly turned into a cough. She turned to Adjoa. 'Sorry. I . . . um . . . thought I saw a rat scrabbling in the straw in Pixie's shelter!'

Adjoa shrugged. 'That's no big deal. The farmer's cats will catch it. Let's go in the house and get a drink.' She opened the field gate that led straight into her back garden.

'OK. I'll follow you in a sec. I think I've got a stone in my boot.' Bending down so that she had her back to Adjoa, Lily beckoned to Storm.

Storm scampered straight over and squeezed under the fence into the back garden. He trotted at Lily's heel, panting happily as they all walked towards the house.

In the kitchen, Adjoa's mum was getting cold drinks from the fridge. 'I saw you coming,' she said, smiling. 'You must be Lily. It's nice to meet you. I'm glad Adjoa's already made a new friend.' Her rows of tiny black plaits were pinned up into a bun. She wore gold hoop earrings, jeans and a pretty green top.

'Thanks for the drink, Mrs Hardiker,' Lily said politely.

After their drinks, Lily and Storm went up to Adjoa's room. 'It's just like mine!' Lily said delightedly, looking at all the pony posters and books. Red and blue rosettes that Adjoa had won for her riding were pinned round her mirror.

'That was brilliant fun! Thanks,'

Lily said to Adjoa, before she left for
home.

'That's OK. You can come here any
time,' Adjoa said, smiling. 'See you at
school on Monday!'

As she walked away with Storm,
Lily was thoughtful. 'Adjoa's mum and
dad don't seem to have a problem with
their daughter looking after a pony
and doing schoolwork. But I don't
think I'll *ever* persuade mine to let
me have one,' she said to him with a
sigh.

Storm whined in sympathy, wagging
his tail. His thick sandy fur gleamed
with tiny golden sparks. 'Maybe I can
help you,' he woofed softly.

★

The following afternoon, Mrs Benson
dropped Lily and Storm off early at
Greengates before she went to her
yoga workshop. Lily had been silently
mulling over what Storm had said;
now she was bursting to ask him
about it.

'Did you mean it, about helping me
to get my own pony?' she asked as they
walked across the stable yard.

Storm looked at her with alert
midnight-blue eyes. 'I did, Lily. I always
keep my promises.'

Lily waited, but Storm didn't say
anything more. Her imagination went
into overdrive. 'I bet you're going to
use your magic to make a pony appear
out of thin air, aren't you? Are you

going to put Mum and Dad into a trance or something, so they let me keep it?' she asked excitedly.

Storm's furry brow dipped in a frown. 'No. That would not be the right thing to do, Lily. I am afraid that you will have to be patient,' he woofed mysteriously. He leapt forward and

went off to explore the yard, shedding a few tiny gold sparks, which glinted in the bright sunlight before dissolving.

Lily stared after Storm. She knew she was going to have to do as he said, but it was hard to be patient when you wanted something so much.

It was time that she went to see what jobs needed doing, but first Lily went to visit Bandit. She had an apple in her pocket for the pony.

But the palomino wasn't in her loose box, so Lily went to check the paddock. Bandit wasn't there either. As she was walking back across the yard feeling puzzled, Don came out of the tack room holding a saddle.

'Is Bandit out on an early ride?' Lily asked the stable lad.

'No. Bandit's already gone. Didn't
Janie tell you?' Don said.

'Gone? Gone where?' Lily asked.

'To her new home,' Don explained.
'Bandit's quite old now and Janie's been
thinking about retiring her for some
time. Someone came by in the week
and offered Bandit a new home on the
spot. Janie jumped at it. Bandit's gone
to live in a field with two goats and a
donkey for company.'

'Oh, she'll really love that,' Lily said,
trying hard not to feel sad. But she
knew she was really going to miss the
gentle old pony.

Don's freckled face crinkled in a
smile. 'It's amazing that somewhere so
perfect came right out of the blue,
when Janie hadn't really started looking

yet. Just like magic, really. Anyway, see you later.' He went off to tack up a pony.

Storm came rushing across the yard, with a dusty nose from where he'd been rooting about in some straw. He gave her a wide doggy grin and flopped down at her feet.

Lily looked down at him thoughtfully. 'Did you have anything to do with finding Bandit a perfect new home, by any chance?'

Storm gave her a cheeky sideways look. He twitched his nose. 'I smell rabbits!' he yapped happily and shot off again towards the paddock.

Lily stared after him. He was up to something, she was sure of it.

Chapter
SIX

It had been another busy afternoon at Greengates. Lily was hanging up a pile of newly cleaned bridles in the tack room.

Janie popped her head round the door. 'Why don't you leave that now and go and have a ride? Tinka's still saddled up.'

'Thanks, Janie!' Glancing over to

where Storm was snoozing on top of
the brush box, Lily called to him.
'Come on, Storm. Walkies!'

'That is my favourite word!' Storm's
head shot up immediately. He jumped
down and padded after Lily to where
Tinka was tied to the hitching rail.

Lily buckled on her riding hat before
mounting the handsome bay pony. She
walked Tinka out of the yard and on to
the bridle path. This time she took the
fork leading to a field that the riding
school had permission to use. Storm

loped along beside her, his ears flapping as Lily rode down a tractor track.

Lily had to concentrate quite hard when riding Tinka. The bay pony was less experienced than dear old Bandit had been. Lily dismounted and was opening the field gate, when a wood pigeon fluttered up out of a bush. Startled, Tinka threw up her head and danced sideways.

'It's OK, girl.' Lily spoke reassuringly, stroking Tinka's nose to calm her.

As Tinka backed up, Lily noticed a ditch almost concealed in the long grass by the hedge. Someone had dumped some sharp hawthorn branches in it. Luckily, Tinka had just missed it or she could have been injured. Lily made a mental note to tell Janie about the dangerous ditch when she got back to Greengates.

Storm sat in her lap as Lily continued her ride. But as she made her way back an hour or so later he loped along beside her once more. She saw him run off into the field and start springing about, barking at butterflies and nosing into molehills. By the time Lily got back to the field gate and dismounted again, Storm was behind her.

Lily led Tinka through and was closing the gate, when she spotted a familiar pony and rider coming towards her along the edge of the field. 'Look, Storm! It's Adjoa on Pixie!' she cried delightedly.

A moist brown nose and then two sandy ears appeared as Storm squeezed

through a small gap in the hedge. He
gave an excited bark and leapt towards
the long grass.

Lily realized that he was heading
straight for the concealed ditch. 'Storm!
Look out!' she cried. But the puppy
was so intent on reaching his friend
Pixie that he didn't seem to have heard
her.

Lily threw herself forward. She missed
Storm, but just managed to push him

sideways as she lost her balance and slid
into the ditch.

'Ow!' she gasped with pain, as her
ankle twisted and sharp thorns dug into
her leg.

Storm looked down at her in dismay.
'You saved me, Lily. But you are hurt. I
will help you,' he whined.

'I . . . I think I'm OK,' Lily said
shakily, biting back tears at the sharp
ache in her leg. Her jodhpurs were torn
and smeared with grass stains.

Time seemed to stand still. Lily felt a
familiar warm tingling down her back
as vivid gold sparks ignited in Storm's
fur. His tail stiffened and crackled with
power. Raising a velvety front paw
Storm sent a whoosh of sparks fizzing
towards Lily's injured leg. For a second

the pain increased and then it drained
away just as if someone had poured it
down a plughole.

When the bright sparks faded,
Lily saw that her jodhpurs were clean
and mended too. 'Thanks, Storm,' she
whispered.

'You are welcome,' Storm woofed as
the final gold sparks faded from his
thick sandy fur.

Lily quickly climbed out of the ditch.
She stood up as Adjoa pulled Pixie to a

halt a couple of metres away. 'Watch out for this ditch. You can hardly see it. I . . . er . . . nearly just slipped right into . . .' she blustered. Lily racked her brain for an explanation that didn't involve Storm, but Adjoa wasn't listening.

Her new friend's eyes were red and puffy. It was obvious that Adjoa had been crying. Lily felt a stir of sympathy. What could be wrong?

Lily held Tinka by her reins and listened with growing dismay to what Adjoa had to say.

'The farmer who we rent Pixie's field from is selling up and we can't find another field nearby. Mum and Dad say it would cost too much to put her into livery stables where she'd be looked after, and so we might have to sell her,' Adjoa said tearfully.

'Oh no! Poor you,' Lily exclaimed, putting one arm round her friend.

She knew it was expensive to have a pony looked after by a livery stable. But it was awful to think of Adjoa losing her beloved pony.

Beside her Pixie gave a friendly blow and dipped her head to nuzzle Storm gently. The tiny puppy was lying on his back in the grass with all four legs in the air, showing his fat pale tummy. For once, Lily felt too upset for Adjoa to smile at his playful antics.

An idea came to her. She was going to talk to her parents.

Chapter
SEVEN

'I'm sorry, Lily. But my answer has to be the same,' Mrs Benson said.

They were all sitting in the kitchen on Saturday evening. Storm was lying down next to Lily's chair, invisible to everyone except her, as usual. Lily had just finished explaining about Pixie in the hope that her parents might be willing to buy the pony.

'I agree with your mum,' Mr Benson said. 'Looking after a pony is a big responsibility. We're just not sure this is the right time for you to take that on.'

'But it is, Dad! I'd be the most brilliant pony owner ever!' Lily said in her best pleading voice. 'And if we bought Pixie, Adjoa could still see her whenever she wanted.'

Her dad smiled and reached out to ruffle her hair. 'I'm sorry, honey. I feel bad for Adjoa too, but the subject's closed.'

'That's what I thought you'd say,' Lily said, sighing heavily.

All that evening and throughout Sunday, Adjoa and Pixie were on Lily's mind. On Monday, when she and Storm walked to school, they met up with Katy and Freema, but Adjoa wasn't with them.

'Where's Adjoa?' Lily asked.

'She's not coming in today. My aunt says she's got an upset tummy,' Freema explained.

'I know *why* Adjoa's tummy is upset. It's because she's so worried about what's going to happen to Pixie,' Lily said sadly.

Freema and Katy nodded.

When they reached the cloakroom, Lily hung back and let her friends go into school ahead of her. 'I wish I could think of a way to help Adjoa keep Pixie,' she whispered to Storm. 'But I've already tried Mum and Dad. I don't know what else I can do.'

Storm whined softly in sympathy and then his big midnight-blue eyes lit up.

'You could talk to the lady who runs the riding stables,' he suggested.

'Janie? I can't see what good that would do,' Lily said, frowning.

Storm barked encouragingly, wagging his tail and dancing round her feet in circles. Lily smiled. 'Well, OK then, if you're that sure it'll help. We'll pop over there tonight after school. Uh-oh! Watch out! Mr Poke's just come in. We'd better go into class!' she hissed out of the side of her mouth.

Back home after school, Lily quickly changed into her jeans and T-shirt, before dashing downstairs. She found her mum in the kitchen. 'Could you give me a lift over to Greengates, please?' she asked.

Her mum looked surprised. 'Don't you get enough of that place at weekends? Why do you want to go over there now?'

Lily thought quickly. 'Tinka was sick on Saturday. I wanted to check and see if she's any better,' she fibbed.

Mrs Benson smiled. 'That's a nice thought. You're a sweet person, Lily Benson.'

Lily blushed, feeling a bit guilty. But there was no way she could tell her mum that it was Storm's suggestion to go and talk to Janie. Anyway, it was true that she was always happy to see Tinka and all the other ponies. 'So can I get a lift?' she prompted.

Her mum nodded. 'We'll go now. I have to go to the supermarket, so I can

drop you off at Greengates and then
pick you up on my way back.'

Lily sat in the back of the car, with
Storm on her lap as they drove there.
She got out of the car at Greengates's
main entrance. 'Thanks for the lift,
Mum. I'll see you later.'

As soon as her mum had driven
away, Lily went into the yard. Storm
trotted purposefully at heel, invisible as
usual.

She could see Janie sitting at her
computer through the office window.

Lily paused, feeling a stir of
uncertainty. 'Well, here I am. But I'm
still not sure why! What am I supposed
to say to her?' she whispered to Storm.

The puppy's luminous midnight-blue
eyes looked even brighter than usual.

'I think you should tell Janie about how Pixie needs a home,' he woofed.

Lily frowned. 'But there's no point. Greengates isn't a livery stable. It's a riding school. And anyway, Janie hasn't got room for any extra ponies. All the loose boxes are full.'

Storm pricked his ears. 'Not all of them.'

Lily blinked as the penny dropped. 'You're right! Bandit's not here any more.'

Storm nodded, looking very pleased with himself.

Before Lily could ask him anything else, Janie came out into the yard. 'Lily? This is a nice surprise. What can I do for you?' she said.

'I . . . um . . .' Lily bit her lip, feeling herself going red as she struggled to find the right words to say. Now that she was here, her mind seemed to have become a complete blank.

Chapter
EIGHT

Storm gave a gentle woof and as Lily
looked down into his sparkling
midnight-blue eyes, she felt herself
starting to calm down.

Lily took a deep breath and suddenly
it all came pouring out. 'I . . . um . . .
wanted to ask you something. I've got a
friend called Adjoa who's got a pony
called Pixie. She's lovely and very

sweet-natured, but the farmer who owns her field is selling up. And I thought, well, I was hoping —'

Janie smiled. 'Whoa! Slow down a bit. Let's go into my office, Lily. I could do with a break from working on my accounts. We'll have a cold drink and you can tell me all about it.'

A few minutes later, Lily sat sipping her apple juice as Janie tapped her fingers on the desk thoughtfully.

'So what you're really asking is for me to put Pixie into livery?' she said to Lily.

Lily nodded, feeling encouraged by Janie's calmness and willingness to listen. Everything seemed to have slotted into place and become clear in her mind. Now Lily knew exactly what to say.

'What about if Pixie lives here *and*
works as one of the riding school
ponies? Adjoa would have to agree, but
I think she'd do anything if it meant
she could keep Pixie. She'd still own
her, so she'd help look after her and pay
towards Pixie's food and bedding and
stuff. But it probably wouldn't cost
anywhere near as much as proper livery.'

'You seem to have got this all worked
out,' Janie said.

'I have!' Lily said firmly.

'Hmm. It could work. We've had arrangements like this in the past and we are a pony short now that Bandit's gone. But I'd have to try Pixie out before I decided that she was right for Greengates. She'd have to be gentle, friendly and dependable.'

'Oh, she is! She's perfect. Shall I ask Adjoa's parents to phone you and fix up a meeting?' Lily asked eagerly.

Janie nodded, smiling. 'Yes. You do that. You're one determined young lady, Lily Benson.'

'That's what my dad says!' Lily beamed at Janie as she got up. 'Thanks so much, Janie. Is it OK if I go and see Tinka and the other ponies? I've just got time before Mum picks me up.'

'Course it is. I'll leave you to it. I'd better get back to these accounts.'

Lily and Storm spent twenty minutes with the ponies before going back to the riding stable's entrance. Mrs Benson had just arrived and was waiting to pick her up.

On the way home in the back of the car, Lily stroked Storm's floppy sandy

ears. 'You had this all worked out, didn't you,' she said softly.

Storm nodded. 'But I could not have done it all by myself. It was you who spoke to Janie. You did it, Lily.'

Lily felt a warm glow of pride. It felt good to have helped her friend. 'I can't wait to tell Adjoa all about it. I'm going to phone her as soon as I get home.'

The moment her mum stopped on the front drive, Lily shot out of the car and made a dash for the house.

'Er, excuse me, young lady! I wouldn't mind a hand with this shopping,' her mum called after her.

'Sorry,' Lily said sheepishly.

She rushed back, grabbed some bags and dumped them on the kitchen table.

As she was coming out of the
kitchen, the hall phone rang.

It was Adjoa's mum. 'Hello, Lily. Is
Adjoa with you? Can I have a word
with her, please?' she asked.

'She isn't here,' Lily replied, puzzled.

'Oh dear, I was hoping she'd ridden
over on Pixie to see you,' Mrs Hardiker
said, sounding worried. 'Could I have a
word with your mum?'

Lily passed the phone over. 'It's Adjoa's mum.'

Lily waited impatiently while the two mums spoke. 'What's going on?' she asked as her mum replaced the phone.

'Adjoa's left a note saying she couldn't bear to give up Pixie, and some of her clothes have gone. Mrs Hardiker was hoping she'd come over here. But it's beginning to look like Adjoa's run away with Pixie.'

'Oh no!' Lily gasped.

Chapter
NINE

'It'll be dark soon. Adjoa must be so scared. We have to find her and tell her the news about Greengates!' Lily said to Storm as soon as they were alone in her bedroom.

Storm nodded. 'I will take us to Adjoa's house and see if I can pick up a fresh trail.'

Lily felt a familiar warm tingling

down her back as gold sparks crackled
in Storm's sandy fur and a fountain
of golden glitter streamed out of his
tail. There was a bright flash and a
whooshing sensation and suddenly Lily
found herself standing with Storm
outside Pixie's field at the back of
Adjoa's house.

Storm sniffed around, picking up
Pixie's scent. Moments later, he
stiffened. Lily saw that his moist brown
nose was glowing like a gold nugget.
'This way!' he barked, setting off at a
run.

Lily followed Storm away from the
field and through the streets. They
hurried along the main road and then
towards the edge of town. The street
lights had already come on. Overhead

the first stars had begun twinkling in
the sky.

Lily grew hot and sweaty as she and
Storm followed Pixie's trail, but she
wasn't tired. Gold sparks flashed past
her as Storm's magic made them
travel in double-quick time. Gradually
Lily realized where they were
heading.

'Greengates is just over there. Adjoa
must have taken the bridle path. I bet
she's planning to hide in the woods
overnight. She'll probably take the
short cut across the fields,' she told
Storm.

A few minutes later, Storm barked
and wagged his tail. 'Over there!'

In the twilight, Lily could just make
out the figure of a pony and rider

against the shadowy hedgerows. The
moon came out from behind a cloud
and Lily could see more clearly. 'It's
them!' she cried.

Lily saw that Pixie was trotting
towards the familiar field gate. 'That
ditch! Adjoa's heading straight for it.
Those prickly branches have been
cleared away since I told Janie about it,
but a pony could still break her leg if
she stumbles into it. I bet she's too

upset to remember it's there and Pixie
won't see it in the dark!'

Storm's midnight-blue eyes flashed.
Another rainbow of sparks shot out
ahead of him and he leapt forward into
the stream of light. Lily felt herself
shooting through the air beside him.
She and Storm landed a few metres in
front of Adjoa and Pixie.

Lily walked forward, holding up her
arms. 'It's me, Lily! Adjoa, Stop!'

Adjoa reined Pixie in. The pony's ears
swivelled and her head came up, but
she halted calmly a few paces away
from the ditch.

'Lily! What are you doing here? How
did you find me?' Adjoa cried.

'Never mind that now,' Lily said. 'That
ditch I fell into the other day is right in

front of you. Pixie could have stumbled into it. Come over here. I have to tell you something.'

Adjoa urged Pixie over to one side, but she didn't dismount. She looked shaken, but determined. 'Thanks for reminding me about that ditch. But if you're going to try and persuade me to go back home, don't bother!' Adjoa said, looking down at Lily.

'Adjoa, listen! I've got some great news,' Lily said quickly before her friend could decide to ride on. 'I've been to see Janie at Greengates. She's willing to take Pixie into livery on condition that you let her be used for the riding school.'

'Really?' Adjoa looked stunned, but her hands loosened on the reins. Her

shoulders relaxed as she thought about it. 'I wouldn't mind little kids riding Pixie and she'd enjoy the extra exercise. Dad said she was getting a bit fat anyway. But even with Janie using Pixie for rides, it's still going to cost quite a lot to keep her stabled at Greengates. I still don't know if Mum and Dad will agree.'

Lily's face fell. She hadn't thought of this. It seemed as if there was a flaw in her brilliant plan.

Storm jumped up with his paws on Lily's leg and woofed for attention. Lily looked down at him. 'You could ask your mum and dad to help,' he suggested in a soft bark.

It was a few seconds before Storm's meaning sank in. 'That's it!' she burst out, her eyes widening.

'What is?' Adjoa said, puzzled.

'I've just had a brilliant idea. Come on, Adjoa. We're going back to talk to my parents!' She quickly outlined her plan.

A look of hope came over Adjoa's face. 'Do you think they'll agree?'

'They have to. It's Pixie's last chance,'

Lily said determinedly turning on her heel, confident that Adjoa would now follow her on Pixie. At her side, Storm gave an encouraging yap.

Chapter
TEN

Later that evening, Lily sat at the kitchen table eating a take-away pizza with her mum and dad. Storm was curled up beneath the table.

'You did well to persuade Adjoa to come home,' her dad said. 'Her parents were almost out of their minds with worry. They've been on the phone singing your praises. Well done, love.'

Lily felt herself blushing. 'Anyone would have done the same.'

'I'm not sure that's true,' her mum said, patting her hand. 'What I still can't work out is how you found her so quickly or got up to the field near Greengates in record time.'

'It must be all the exercise I've been doing. I'm super-fit, aren't I, Dad? Mmm. This pizza's delish!' Lily said, quickly changing the subject. She slipped a small piece under the table for Storm to munch. 'Mu–um? Da–ad?' she said in a wheedling voice. 'I've . . . um . . . got something to ask you.'

Her parents exchanged glances. 'I hope this isn't about having your own pony again!' Mrs Benson said.

'Course it's not,' Lily said brightly.

'Thank goodness for that!' her dad said.

Lily paused for effect. 'It's about me having half a pony!'

Mr Benson frowned. 'Run that by me again.'

Lily grinned. 'What I really mean is *sharing* a pony!' She explained about Janie agreeing to take Pixie into livery and being a riding school pony. 'But it's still going to be quite expensive, so

Adjoa's parents might decide to sell Pixie anyway. But they won't if we help with the costs. And then I'd be sort of sharing a pony with Adjoa. I'd be able to groom Pixie and ride her sometimes. What do you think?'

'I think Pixie's going to be one busy pony!' her dad said, smiling. 'But it's an interesting idea.'

Lily held her breath and had all her fingers and toes crossed. At least her dad hadn't said no outright like he usually did.

'I know you, Lily. You'll want to be up at Greengates every night, looking after Pixie and grooming her,' said Mrs Benson. 'I'm still worried that your schoolwork could suffer.'

'I know I might like to do that, but I

won't, because I'll know that I have to take turns with Adjoa,' Lily said honestly. 'I'll just be so happy to be able to ride Pixie sometimes – and pretend she's all mine until I get a pony of my own one day!'

Her mum and dad exchanged glances.

'Well, when you put it like that, it sounds like a sensible arrangement,' her mum said.

'And it's the only way Lily's ever going to give us any peace! So the answer's yes,' her dad added.

'Yay!' Lily flung herself at her parents and gave them both huge hugs and then did a little dance around the table. 'I can't wait to tell Adjoa!'

Storm ran out from under the table and jumped up and down, barking

excitedly. Lily grinned and only just
managed to stop herself from bending
down and picking him up.

Later that night, Lily closed her
bedroom curtains, getting ready for bed.
Outside in the street she saw a
couple of people taking their dogs for a

last walk. She jumped into bed and snuggled up under the duvet with Storm.

'Thanks so much for everything, Storm. You kept your promise about helping me to get a pony, even though things turned out differently to how I imagined! You're the most brilliant friend ever. We're going to have an amazing summer with Pixie and Adjoa!'

Storm tucked his head under her chin. 'I am glad I was able to help.'

Suddenly Lily heard howling and growling from outside in the street. She jumped back out of bed and peered through the bedroom curtains. The two dog walkers were struggling to control their dogs, which were straining at their leads and looking up at her bedroom.

In the light of the street lamps, the dogs' eyes looked pale and were glowing.

'That's weird . . .' Lily said, turning to Storm.

The tiny puppy was cowering in the bed. She could see him trembling with fright.

Frowning, Lily glanced outside again and saw the dogs suddenly calm down. After a moment, their puzzled owners walked on until they were out of sight.

Lily came back to Storm. As she went to stroke him she realized that he was trembling all over. 'What's wrong? Are you sick?' she asked worriedly.

Storm shook his head. His ears were laid back and his tail was tucked

beneath him. 'I sense that Shadow is
close. I think he used his magic, so that
the dogs outside would attack me.'

Lily looked at her friend in dismay. 'Is
that what he'll do if he finds you?

Storm nodded, his eyes as dull as blue
stones. 'All the dogs around here will be
looking for me now. I will use my
magic to mask my scent. It may give
me a little more time.'

Lily kissed the top of his sandy head,

breathing in his sweet puppy smell, and
lay awake, hoping like mad that Storm
would be safe. She didn't think she
could bear it if she never saw him
again.

Chapter
ELEVEN

Lily woke with a start the next morning. To her relief, Storm was curled up asleep next to her.

He seemed more like his normal self, but his sparkling midnight-blue eyes were still wary. 'I will stay here and hide. I want to be sure that Shadow cannot sense where I am,' he barked.

Lily felt reluctant to leave him, but

she had promised to meet Adjoa at
Greengates and help settle Pixie into
her new home.

'I'll see you later,' she said, bending
down to kiss the top of Storm's warm
silky head.

Storm curled himself into a tight ball
and didn't answer.

'Whoa, there, girl!' Janie Green said
gently.

Lily and Adjoa stood watching as
Janie backed Pixie out of the horse
trailer, hitched to her Land Rover.
'That's it; good. Come on.'

Pixie slowly moved backwards, step
by step. Finally she stood in the stable
yard, her legs trembling slightly and her
chestnut coat twitching.

'Good girl,' Adjoa crooned, going over to stroke Pixie's nose. 'She's feeling nervous. She's been used to living in a field by herself.'

'It's only natural for her to feel un-settled,' Janie said understandingly. 'She's used to you, so why don't you and Lily lead her around for a bit before you take her in to the loose box? Call me if you have any problems. OK?'

'OK. Thanks.' Adjoa looked over at Lily as Janie went to park her Land Rover. 'Janie's really nice, isn't she?'

Lily smiled and nodded. 'There are lots of strange new smells here. Why don't you walk Pixie past the paddock a few times? It might calm her if she smells fresh grass like in her field,' she suggested to Adjoa.

'That's a good idea.'

For the next twenty minutes Adjoa led Pixie round the yard, talking gently to her all the time.

Lily watched, trying not to think about Storm and whether he was still safe. But her worries about her tiny puppy friend kept pushing into her mind.

Pixie gradually seemed to relax.

Finally, Adjoa felt confident enough to lead her to Bandit's old loose box, which was to be her new home. Earlier, Lily had spread it with a deep layer of clean bedding. There was a hay net hanging up and clean water in a bucket.

Lily opened the door wide.

Adjoa went to lead Pixie inside. But Pixie rolled her eyes and stood still. 'Come on. It's lovely in there. There's space for you to turn round and lie down if you want to,' she encouraged.

Pixie shifted nervously and rolled her eyes. 'She's just not keen on going indoors,' Adjoa said.

'I'll get a bit of carrot from the feed store. That might tempt her in,' Lily said.

'Good idea,' Adjoa said gratefully.

Lily returned quickly. But the carrot didn't work either.

'What if we can't get Pixie to go in at all?' Adjoa said worriedly. 'Janie might change her mind about her. She won't want an awkward pony at the riding school.'

'That's not going to happen. Pixie's just scared. She's going to be fine,' Lily said reassuringly, but she was starting to get concerned.

If only Storm was here. He'd calm Pixie down. But Storm had to fight his own battle, hiding from his enemy – the fierce wolf Shadow.

'I think I'd better go and get Janie or Don, after all,' Lily decided reluctantly after another fifteen minutes of leading

Pixie about and a second failed attempt at getting her to go into her box.

'OK, then.' Adjoa was almost in tears.

Just then Lily heard a rustling sound from inside the loose box. A spurt of bright golden sparks shot up out of the straw and a cheeky sandy face appeared.

'Storm!' Lily exclaimed delightedly and then realized that Adjoa was giving her a strange look. 'I mean . . . it looks like rain or something. I think we should try Pixie once more before we go and get help.'

Adjoa looked doubtful, but she nodded.

Pixie stretched out her neck and blew a warm breath towards Storm. Storm barked encouragingly and wagged his tail.

Pixie lifted one front leg. She took a step forward and then another one. She went inside and Adjoa closed the door after her. 'Phew! At last! I thought she'd never go in,' she said, relieved.

'She'll be fine now. Why don't you go and tell Janie?' Lily suggested.

Just as Adjoa disappeared into the office, Storm whined in terror. He leapt over the stable door into the yard, trailing a bright comet's tail of golden sparks and streaked towards the tack room.

Lily whipped round and saw two small dogs coming through the main gates. They raised their heads and she saw their abnormally long teeth and fierce pale wolf eyes. Her heart missed a beat. They were here for Storm!

She dashed across the yard and rushed into the empty tack room.

There was a bright golden flash. Lily blinked hard as her sight cleared. Storm stood there as his magnificent real self. The majestic young wolf's dazzling silver-grey fur gleamed and his midnight-blue eyes glowed like sapphires. A she-wolf with a gentle tired face stood next to Storm.

And then Lily knew that this time Storm was leaving for good.

'Our enemies are very close. We must go!' Storm's mother rumbled.

Storm raised a large silver paw in farewell. 'You have been a good friend. Be of good heart, Lily,' he said in a deep velvety growl.

Lily's throat closed with tears and there was an ache in her chest. She was going to miss Storm terribly. 'Goodbye,

Storm. Take care. I'll never forget you,'
she whispered hoarsely.

There was a final bright flash and a
crackle of gold sparks that sprinkled
down around her like warm rain.
Storm and his mother faded and then
disappeared. The dogs ran into the tack
room. Lily saw their teeth and eyes
instantly return to normal before they
turned and slunk away.

Lily blinked away tears as she went
slowly back out into the yard. At least
she'd had a chance to say goodbye to
Storm. She knew she'd never forget the
wonderful adventure she'd shared with
the magic puppy.

Although she could never tell another
person about Storm, there was someone
else who was going to miss the tiny

puppy and with whom she could share all her thoughts. Pixie!

As Lily went towards Pixie's stall and saw Adjoa coming out of Janie's office, she smiled at the thought of all the adventures they were going to have with their very own pony!

Win a Magic Puppy goody bag!

The evil wolf Shadow has ripped out part of Storm's
letter from his mother and hidden the words so that magic puppy
Storm can't find them.

Storm needs your help!

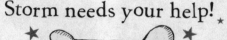

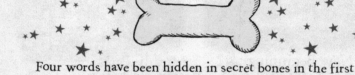

Four words have been hidden in secret bones in the first
four Magic Puppy books. Find the hidden words and put them
together to complete the message from Storm's mother.
Send it in to us and each month we will put every correct message
in a draw and pick out one lucky winner, who will receive
a Magic Puppy gift – definitely worth barking about!

Send the hidden message, your name and address on a postcard to:
Magic Puppy Competition
Puffin Books
80 Strand
London WC2R 0RL
Good luck!

puffin.co.uk

Magic Puppy

A New Beginning
★ 9780141323503 ★

Muddy Paws
9780141323510

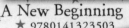

Cloud Capers
9780141323527

Star of the Show
9780141323534

puffin.co.uk

Coming Soon

A little puppy,
a sprinkling of magic,
a forever friend.

If you like
Magic Puppy,
you'll love

Magic Kitten

A Summer Spell
9780141320144

Classroom Chaos
9780141320151

Star Dreams
9780141320168

Double Trouble
9780141320175

Moonlight Mischief
9780141321530

A Circus Wish
9780141321547

Sparkling Steps
9780141321554

A Glittering Gallop
9780141321561

Seaside Mystery
9780141321981

Firelight Friends
9780141321998

Sparkling Steps
9780141321554

A Puzzle of Paws
9780141322018

A Christmas Surprise
9780141323237

Picture Perfect
9780141323480

A Splash of Forever
9780141323497